Loads of Laughs

First U.S. edition 2019

First published by Black Dog Books,
an imprint of Walker Books Australia Pty Ltd 2017

Library of Congress Catalog Card Number 2019939646
ISBN 978-1-5362-0914-3

19 20 21 22 23 24 LBM 10 9 8 7 6 5 4 3 2 1

Printed in Melrose Park, IL, U.S.A.

This book was typeset in New Century Schoolbook and Love Ya Like a Sister.
The illustrations were done in pen and ink.

Candlewick Entertainment
an imprint of
Candlewick Press
99 Dover Street
Somerville, Massachusetts 02144

visit us at www.candlewick.com

Little Lunch

Loads of Laughs

Danny Katz
illustrated by Mitch Vane

**CANDLEWICK
ENTERTAINMENT**

BATTIE
gentle
creative
imaginative

ATTICUS
sweet
curious
always hungry

DEBRA-JO

smart

ambitious

organized

MELANIE

determined

courageous

shy

RORY
mischievous
easily distracted
liked by everyone

TAMARA
athletic
energetic
confident

MRS. GONSHA

extremely patient
(with a tendency
to nod off in class)

The Ya-Ya

On Monday morning at little lunch,
Atticus sat down. Opened his blue
lunch box. Looked inside. Slammed
it shut again. Then just sat there,
making a disgusted face
like he'd drunk a whole
jar of dirty art room
paintbrush-cleaning
water.

SLURP
SLURP

On Tuesday
morning, Atticus sat
down at little lunch.
Opened his
blue lunch box. Looked
inside. Slammed it shut
again. Made an even
more disgusted face, like
he'd sniffed a pair of Tamara
Noodle's sports socks right
after a field day.

On Wednesday
morning, it
happened again.
Atticus sat down
at little lunch, opened his blue lunch
box, looked inside, slammed it shut.

He made the
most disgusted
face anyone could
make, like he'd
licked a garbage
can. The *inside* of
a garbage can. Right down at the
bottom where
all the **goopy** stuff goes.

Usually Atticus loved eating
food at little lunch. He loved
eating food more than anything.

What was going on? Was he
feeling sick? Was he on a diet?
Was there something inside the
lunch box that was freaking
him out?

3

Maybe there was
a family of cockroaches
running around in there.

Or an angry rat, curled
up in the corner?

Only Atticus
knew the truth.
And the truth
was his parents
had gone away for
a week. His mom had a work
conference in New Zealand, and his
dad had never been to New Zealand,
so his dad went too. Which meant . . .
Atticus had to be looked after by
his . . .

ya-ya.

4

yo-yo
YA-YA!

A ya-ya is not a small round toy that spins on a string— that's a yo-yo. And a ya-ya is not what cowboys yell out to their horses—that's "Yah YAHHHH!" And a ya-ya is not what you say when your parents tell you to clean your room and you're not really listening. That's "Yeahhhh . . . yeahhhhhhhh . . ."

Ya-Ya is the name Atticus calls his grandmother. Because his grandmother comes from a country where all grandmothers are called Ya-Ya.

yo-yo
YEAH-YEAH!

A country far, far away . . . where they make lunches that smell really weird.

Atticus loved everything about his ya-ya, except for her cooking. And all week long she'd been putting some pretty weird food in his lunch box. It was always the same small, brown, smelly wrap things. They looked bad, they smelled strange, and he had no idea what they even *were*. Were they made from some kind of vegetable that had been pickled in a jar for a hundred years?

Were they made out of

HOW OLD ARE YOU? I'M ONLY 90

meat from an animal that people don't normally eat? A bear? Or a mongoose? Or something slimy that lived in a swamp?

All he knew for sure was he didn't want to eat those small, brown,

SMELLY

wrap things. Why couldn't his ya-ya give him normal lunch box food like his parents always gave him?

Something
simple and
delicious like
a cheese stick or some slices of
bread and butter. Something that
didn't look like it had been scraped
off the bottom of someone's shoe
after a walk in
a dog park.

What made
the lunch box
problem way, way
worse was . . . when
Atticus didn't eat, he got hungry, and
when he got hungry, he got

grumpy.

VERY GRUMPY.

For the last few days he'd been snapping at his friends for no good reason at all. Just yesterday he was sitting next to Melanie in art class, and he yelled at her, "WHO SAID YOU COULD USE MY PENCIL, MELANIE?"

"This is *my* pencil," she told him.

Atticus yelled again, "HOW CAN YOU BE SO SURE?"

Melanie held up the pencil. "Because it's pink with unicorns and sparkles and has my name written on the side!"

Atticus kept yelling. "OK, THEN! I'M SORRY FOR MAKING A MISTAKE! KEEP DRAWING! THAT'S A NICE DRAWING OF A PARROT BY THE WAY! REALLY GOOD WORK, MELANIE!"

On Thursday morning, Atticus sat down at little lunch. Opened his blue lunch box. Looked inside. Yep, the same small, brown, **smelly** wrap things. He didn't know what to do with them, so he sneaked over to the school worm farm beside the teachers' parking lot and secretly dumped them into a worm bin.

INCOMING!

"Sorry, worms," he whispered into the bin. "I hope this doesn't kill you. If it does, don't blame me. Blame my ya-ya."

Friday was Friday Treat Day, when everyone was allowed to bring their favorite treats to school. Atticus didn't bring his blue lunch box to school with him—he left it at home accidentally-on-purposely.

Then when everyone sat down for little lunch, he put on a fake-shocked face and said, "**Oh, no!** I left my lunch box at home! I have nothing to eat today! What am I going to do?"

He even fake-sniffled like he was really sad. It was a nice touch and it totally worked.

All his friends felt bad for him and shared their favorite Friday treats.

Two chocolate cookies from Melanie.

Half a pastry from Debra-Jo.

A vegetarian pizza slice from Tamara.

A whole sausage roll from Battie.

YAYYYYYY, Battie!

← 1 WHOLE SAUSAGE ROLL

And a ham-and-honey sandwich from Rory.

← 1 HAM and HONEY sandwich

It actually looked kind of disgusting, but Atticus took it anyway—a ham-and-honey sandwich would have to taste better than smelly brown wrap things that might be made from something slimy that once lived in a swamp.

Gathering up all the food in his arms, he scurried away to eat by himself around the corner. He was

extremely

hungry and he didn't want anyone to see him eat — he was planning on eating very, very fast, and it wasn't going to be pretty.

He sat on a step and started with Battie's sausage roll. Here we go, here we go: *real food, good food, deeeee-licious food . . .*

He jammed it in his mouth.

"Atticus!" Mrs. Gonsha hurried toward him, holding something in her hands.

Something blue.

Something shaped like a lunch box.

Something that looked very much like his blue lunch box that he'd accidentally-on-purposely left at home.

"You forgot your lunch box!" she called out. "Your grandmother just dropped it off!"

Atticus's mouth fell open. The sausage roll fell out at the same time.

Mrs. Gonsha plonked the blue lunch box on the step next to Atticus. "There you go! And that's not all your grandmother dropped off! She brought in extra food for all of us!"

Uh-oh. Debra-Jo was walking toward him carrying . . . a silver tray covered in foil.

Following behind her was Tamara carrying . . . *another* silver tray covered in foil.

Next came Melanie, carrying . . . whaaa? . . . a *third* tray covered in foil!

And right at the back were Rory and Battie, carrying nothing, just following the food smells that were coming out of the three silver trays.

It was a big smelly Ya-Ya Food Parade!

This was like a nightmare—a nightmare you couldn't wake up from. It was one thing for Atticus not to like his ya-ya's food and make a **disgusted** face. But he didn't want everyone else not to like his ya-ya's food and make disgusted faces!

This could turn out to be the most embarrassing moment of his life.

"What a lovely, generous thing for your grandmother to do!" said Mrs. Gonsha as the girls put the foil trays on the step beside Atticus. Everyone gathered close, wanting to see what was inside, waiting for Mrs. Gonsha to lift off the foil.

Atticus jumped to his feet.

"Wait, Mrs. Gonsha! You can't let everyone eat that!"

They all turned to look at him, surprised.

"Why not?" asked Mrs. Gonsha.

"Because . . . because . . ."

What could he say? Because it's disgusting? Because it **smells bad**? Because it looks like something that was scraped off the bottom of a shoe?

"Because my ya-ya doesn't know about allergies! There might be **nuts!**"

"There are no nuts," said Mrs. Gonsha, smiling. "She told me the ingredients."

"Are you sure? What about gluten? Lactose? Fructose? . . . Cellulose?"

"Atticus, it's fine! Let's dig in, everybody!"

Mrs. Gonsha lifted the foil off the three silver trays.

The kids peered inside.

Nobody could explain what it was.

Nobody knew how to describe it.

Nobody had ever seen anything like it.

Atticus slumped on the steps and dropped his head in his hands. *Thanks, Ya-Ya.*

Thanks a lot. This is the most embarrassing moment of my life, and it's all because of—

"Yummmmmmm!"

Rory had a small, brown, smelly wrap thing stuffed in his mouth. And he actually seemed to be *liking* it.

But that didn't mean anything. It was Rory. He ate honey-and-ham sandwiches.

"Hmmmm-HMMMM."
Tamara was biting into one.

"This is sooo good! Isn't it, Mrs. Gonsha?"

Mrs. Gonsha couldn't answer.
She was enjoying her small, brown,
smelly wrap thing so much, she
was eating with her eyes closed,
savoring every bite.

Debra-Jo, Battie, and Melanie
were all eating, smiling, and making
Hmmmmmm noises!

What was going on here?
Mrs. Gonsha licked her fingers.

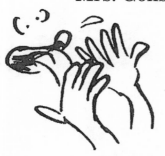

"Your ya-ya is a very,
very special woman,
Atticus! What a cook!"

Debra-Jo grabbed
another one from
a tray. "Atticus, can your ya-ya
give Mrs. Gonsha the recipe so we

can put it on our classroom food blog?"

Battie grabbed a couple, holding one out to Atticus. "Here, Atticus. Aren't you going to have one?"

The small, brown, smelly wrap thing hovered in the air before Atticus. The thing is . . .

The fact is . . .

He'd never actually *eaten* any of Ya-Ya's food. He just didn't like the *look* of it. So he assumed it would taste bad, too.

He took it from Battie's hand.

Studied it up close.

Nibbled a tiny bit from one end.

OK, it wasn't *completely* disgusting.

A bigger nibble.

Not so disgusting at all.

Popped the whole thing in his mouth.

You know what?

It was sort of . . . **tasty.**

It was sweet. It was spicy. It was tangy. It was salty. It was crisp. It was juicy. It was yummy. It was scrummy. And when he went to grab another one, it was . . . all gone.

The three trays were empty.

Everyone was walking away, their hands full of small, brown, smelly wrap things to eat later. Mrs. Gonsha had about twenty-five of them, balancing them in her hands like a wobbly tower.

Arghhhhh!

Atticus was furious with himself. He'd wasted the whole week not wanting to eat his ya-ya's food, and now all he wanted to do was eat his ya-ya's food.

But there was **none** left.

All he had to eat were the Friday treats his friends had given him. The boring chocolate cookies. The tasteless pastry. That soggy slice of pizza. The rest of Battie's cold

sausage roll. And Rory's gross ham-and-honey sandwich.

Just thinking about it made Atticus's stomach flip around.

He didn't want normal food anymore. He wanted weird, smelly Ya-Ya food.

On the edge of the step he noticed something blue.

Oh, yeah! He'd totally forgotten. His ya-ya had brought in his lunch box from home!

He picked it up, opened the lid, and looked inside.

Woohooooo!!!!!

It was stuffed full of small, brown, smelly wrap things.

He popped three into his mouth at the same time, and as he chewed, he thought about how nice it was going to be to have his mom and dad home  from New Zealand after their week away. And he was going to ask if his ya-ya could stay a little bit longer, like for the whole weekend.

And do lots and lots and lots of cooking.

Atticus ate everything in his lunch box, and when the bell rang, he stuck his face inside and licked up every last leftover scrap.

On his way back to class, he made a quick stop at the worm farm to throw in the pastry, the pizza slice, the chocolate cookies, and the rest of the sausage roll.

But not Rory's honey-and-ham sandwich.

No worm deserves to suffer like that. EVER.

The Dress-Up Day

Today was "Dress Up as What You Want to Be When You Grow Up" Day.

Tamara Noodle came to school dressed as a world champion athlete. She wore a green-and-gold tracksuit top and green-and-gold tracksuit bottoms. She also wore her dad's watch on her wrist, because not only did she want to be a world champion athlete; she wanted to be a world champion athlete who had a sponsorship deal with a watch company.

Atticus loved food, so he came to school dressed in a chef's outfit.

He had a big white chef's hat and a white button-up chef's coat, and he drew a little curly mustache on his face. The mustache had nothing to do with being a chef. He just planned on growing a mustache one day, and he wanted to see how it looked.

Debra-Jo always dreamed that one day she'd be a lawyer or the principal of an art school. Those were **boring** costumes, so she borrowed her mom's surgical scrubs and came to school dressed as a doctor instead. A doctor who hates the sight of blood and would much rather be a lawyer or the principal of an art school.

Melanie loved animals, so she decided to dress up as a vet, but she didn't know what kind of uniform a vet wears, so she threw on an old kitchen apron.

That made her look like a waitress, so she panicked and brought her dog, Rudy, to school with her as well. That didn't help either—**dogs were not allowed** on school grounds. So Rudy had to be tied up outside, and Melanie spent the day looking like a waitress.

Rory completely forgot it was "Dress Up as What You Want to Be When You Grow Up" Day.

He only realized when he arrived

at the school gates and saw everyone else dressed up. So he borrowed the crossing guard's white coat and spiked up his hair with a bit of spit. When he walked into school, Atticus said, "Hey, Rory, are you a scientist?" And Rory said, "Oh . . . OK then . . . I'm a scientist."

Battie came to school dressed as Stretcho—a superhero he had made up himself. He knew he wasn't going to be a superhero when he grew up, but he liked to dress up as one. He did it for any kind of school dress-up day, and also friends' dress-up parties, and sometimes just when he was sitting at home watching TV.

He even had a whole 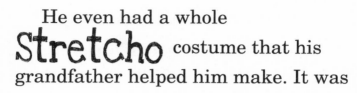 **Stretcho** costume that his grandfather helped him make. It was a brown puffy jacket with a round metal helmet and a floppy rubber arm that could stretch and stretch for ages.

The rubber arm looked really cool when it was stretching

and a little **weird** when it was hanging by his side, like a thick, floppy garden hose with fingers on the end.

Whenever Battie wore his Stretcho suit, he felt powerful and  brave and strong, even though he wasn't really like that at all—he was kind of shy and skinny and

scared of lots of things!

Moths

Crabs

Escalators

Needles

Bees

Cotton balls

Yes, even cotton balls. He didn't like the feel of them. It made him go *hh-hh-hh-hh-hh-hh*.

But today, dressed up as Stretcho, he felt completely fearless and ready to do some good superhero deeds.

At the start of little lunch, he headed straight

38

for Stretcho's secret headquarters—
the old shed. Then he stood
on the bench and scanned the
schoolyard, looking for innocent
people who needed to be saved or
evil supervillains who needed to be
defeated.

Aha! An evil supervillain was
passing right now! It was Rory in
his scientist crossing guard outfit.

Stretcho leaped in
front of
him,
holding
out his
stretchy
arm.

RADIOACTIVE

HEH HEH

SCIENTIST
(EVIL)

"Stop, evil scientist! It falls upon me to defend our city from your apocalyptic intentions!"

Rory just stood there. He didn't understand a word Battie had said.

"I'll ask again!" said Battie. "Will you relinquish the ballistic sonic-ray blaster?"

Rory shrugged. Who was Ray Blaster?

Something caught Battie's attention near the spigot. He said, "Excuse me, evil 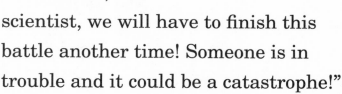 scientist, we will have to finish this battle another time! Someone is in trouble and it could be a catastrophe!"

Sprinting across the playground at super-Stretcho speed, Battie arrived at the spigot, where Melanie was filling up her water bottle.

"Hey, waitress, stop!" he shouted in his bravest superhero voice. "An evil scientist has contaminated this water with radioactive filtration!"

"I'm not a waitress!" Melanie snapped. "I'm a vet!"

"Hmmmm!" said Battie, tapping his chin with his Stretcho hand. "Or are you a waitress who's inhaled radioactive fumes and you've been brainwashed into thinking you're a vet? In which case . . . I must save you!"

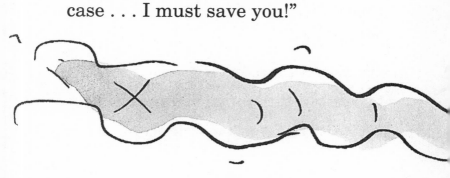

He grabbed her water bottle with his Stretcho hand, but Melanie held tight. "Let go! I need to fill up my water bottle so I can give Rudy a drink!"

Battie pulled harder, the arm stretching longer. "No, waitress, I have to save you from danger!"

"No, you don't!" Melanie yanked her water bottle away from his rubber fingers. "And I'm **not** a waitress! I'm a vet!"

She stormed off toward the school gate.

Battie stood and
watched her go, his
rubber arm dangling
by his side. But he
didn't have to stand
there for long. Someone
else needed help, over on the
monkey bars!

Tamara was hanging upside-down
from her knees, enjoying the view.

She'd been hanging
like that since the
start of little lunch,
lifting her head up
every thirty
seconds to stop
all the blood

from rushing to her brain. She
timed it exactly, using her dad's
watch.

Battie's face appeared before her.
"Don't move, Tamara! Stretcho will
save you!"

He wrapped his
stretchy arm
around and
around her
head. "Now, tell
me! Who did this
to you? Who
suspended you
above the vat
of poisonous
snakes?"

"What snakes?" said Tamara, wriggling her head free, trying to see if there were any snakes down below.

"No time for questions!" said Battie. "The timer will go off in exactly seventy-eight seconds, and you will **plunge** into the snake vat! Can't you hear the ticking?"

TICK TICK TICK TICK

"Oh, that? That's my dad's watch." Tamara waved her watch in Battie's face. "He let me borrow it because that's what I'm going to be when I grow up: a world champion athlete with a sponsorship deal."

Battie was
getting frustrated.
"Come on, Tamara.
Just pretend
there's a detonator

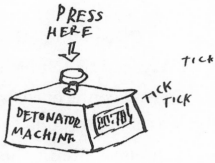

PRESS
HERE

DETONATOR
MACHINE

TICK
TICK
TICK
TICK

machine about to go off and I need
to **Save** you!"

Tamara
squeezed her
head free
from his
rubber
arm,
flipped
herself

right way up, and sat sideways on
the top of the monkey bars.

"I've got a better game, Battie! You can watch me do my athlete's press conference!"

She pretended there were TV cameras filming her, then smiled and said, "Well . . . I felt **great** in the lead-up to the race. I tried to stay focused. I really dug deep. I came out here to defend my title, and I really felt I delivered today!"

She smiled a gold-winning smile and winked at the cameras.

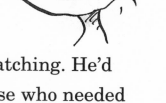

Battie wasn't watching. He'd spotted someone else who needed help, and there was no time to waste!

Sitting on a school
step, Debra-Jo was
drawing a picture with markers.
Battie raced over and jumped in
front of her, knocking her hand with
his shoe, making her scrawl

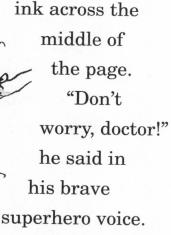

ink across the
middle of
the page.
"Don't
worry, doctor!"
he said in
his brave
superhero voice.
"Stretcho is here! I will stop you from
falling off the edge of this dangerous
skyscraper!"

Debra-Jo shrieked.
"Battie! Look! You
wrecked my picture!
Do I jump on you
when you're making
a sculpture out of sticks? No.

Do I jump on
you when you're
laying out your
raisins in a
pattern? No.

Do I jump on
you when
you're doing
that creepy face
and talking to
a tree? No.

SO DON'T JUMP ON ME!!!!!"

She grabbed all her colored markers, picked up her ruined picture, scowled at him, and then stomped off.

Feeling unwanted, Battie shuffled back to Stretcho's secret headquarters and slumped on his bench.

The trouble with playing imaginary superhero games with his friends was that they didn't always play along.

Maybe he should just play his imaginary superhero games by himself.

He sat and he thought and he began to create a new story starring Stretcho. He had an excellent idea. It was about Stretcho when he was a baby. How Stretcho was born in a hospital and . . . in that same hospital, there was a killer virus—

"Battie?" Debra-Jo popped her head into Stretcho's secret headquarters, breaking his train of thought.

"Listen. I'm sorry for yelling at you before. It's just a picture and I shouldn't have gotten so mad."

"That's OK," said Battie. "Sorry for wrecking your art."

Debra-Jo was pleased that he said that. "Yes," she said, walking away, "it *is* art. Thank you for noticing!"

When she'd gone, Battie took a deep breath and tried to re-enter the imaginary world of his superhero. OK . . . so somehow the killer virus got into the hospital air-conditioning duct and it—

"Hi, Battie." Melanie sat down next to him. "Sorry for getting so

mad at you at the spigot.
I mean, you were
pretty ridiculous
thinking I was a waitress,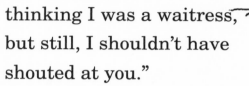
but still, I shouldn't have
shouted at you."

"That's OK," said Battie.

"What are you doing?"

"Just thinking."

"Want to do something?"

"Nah," said Battie.

Melanie shrugged, stood up,
and left.

Back to the story: the killer
virus traveled through the air-
conditioning duct all the way to

the room where baby Stretcho was
sleeping and then—

"Hey, Battie." Tamara
had come over. "Let's see
who's the fastest in a race—
Stretcho or the world champion
athlete with a sponsorship!"

"Well, I'm actually a bit
busy, Tamara. I'm thinking
up a story in my head."

"Cool. What's it about?"

"It's about Stretcho."

"Cool. So what happens?"

"Well, it starts when Stretcho
is born, in a hospital, and there's a—"

"Cool. Do you want to watch me do
cartwheels?"

Before he could answer, she started doing cartwheels in front of him, **one after the other after the other** until she cartwheeled off into the distance and he couldn't see her anymore.

What was going on?

When he wanted to play with his friends, no one wanted to join in on the game. When he sat still by himself, they wouldn't leave him alone.

Battie closed his eyes to concentrate and tried to get back into the story.

OK . . . one tiny
little drop of killer
virus dribbled out
of the air-conditioning
duct and dripped
on Stretcho's
arm. It was too
tiny to kill him,
but it did something
else. It turned his arm into a
powerful, amazing, stretchy—

What was that?

Something furry touched Battie's
leg. At first he thought it might be
Rory, but when he opened his eyes
and looked down . . .

It wasn't Rory.

It was a *dog.*

Melanie's dog.

Melanie was supposed to tie her dog up outside the school grounds. Somehow the dog must have gotten free and was now sitting at Battie's feet, looking up at him with its cute doggy face, blinking its cute doggy eyes.

Battie was scared of lots of things.

Needles Moths Escalators
Bees Cotton balls Crabs

But most of all . . . dogs.

Even cute ones with furry, waggly tails.

The dog stared up at him.

He peeked down at the dog.
He tried to be brave. He tried to be
fearless. He reminded himself that
he was Stretcho and he wasn't
scared of anything!

The dog jumped
up on his lap.
"HELP!
SOMEBODY! A
DOG! HELP!"

HELLLP!!!

Battie's screams were so loud, kids across the playground turned to look. Flocks of birds flew out of trees. Mrs. Gonsha even heard him from the staff room, on the other side of the school, with the windows closed.

"HELP! A DOG! SOMEONE!"

That's Battie, thought Mrs. Gonsha. *And it sounds like he's in trouble!*

She immediately raced out of the staff room, down the hall, out the main doors, and across the playgrounds, both junior and senior. She found Battie in the shed with the dog on his lap, shaking in fear and holding his Stretcho arm over his face for protection.

"It's all right, Battie. It's all right," she said, lifting the dog off his lap. "He won't hurt you. It's just a dog."

Mrs. Gonsha bravely carried the dog away. She was a true superhero. She was . . .

MRS. SUPER GONSHA

When Battie was completely sure that the dog was gone, he peered out from behind his Stretcho arm.

OK, so he was definitely not as brave and strong and powerful as he'd like to be. But that was all right. Every superhero had something they were scared of. Stretcho just had a few more things than most.

Crabs

Moths

Bees

 Needles

Dogs

Cotton balls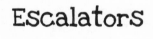

Escalators

Snakes

Cats,

      deep water,

            shallow water.

And knees.

Yep, even knees.

Sometimes they looked like scary little faces. . . .

Knees

The Germblock

Oh boy, oh boy, oh boy. Melanie was excited. *Oh boy, oh boy, oh boy.* This was going to be the best little lunch!

As soon as the bell rang for little lunch, she ran to the girls' bathroom and took a quick pee. Then she raced across the asphalt to her favorite bench beside the redbrick wall. She quickly sat down and popped open the lid of her lunch box.

YUMMMMMMM!

A big slice of leftover cake from her little brother's birthday.

STRAWBERRY

CHOCOLATE CANDIES

CHOCOLATE FROSTING

CHOCOLATE FUDGE

CHOCOLICIOUS!

It was a chocolate cake with chocolate fudge in the middle, chocolate frosting on the top, chocolate candies all over the top, and a little slice of strawberry right in the middle to balance out all the chocolatey-ness.

Oh boy, oh boy, oh boy.
Melanie had been
dreaming of this
moment all morning.
She picked up the
slice, brought it up
to her mouth, and prepared to
plunge into

ultra-choco-happiness. . . .

"GERMBLOCK!"
Tamara Noodle was standing

in front of her,
crossing her
arms in a
gigantic X.

Then Atticus
appeared out of
nowhere, yelled
"Germblock!" and crossed his
arms in an X too.

Debra-Jo ran
over, crossed her
arms, and yelled
"Germblock!"

Battie joined in.
"Germblock!" he yelled,
crossing his arms.

Last of all Rory showed up, yelled
"Germblock!" crossed his
arms, did a monkey squat, and made
a wet tooty sound with his lips:
TRRRRRTTT. He had his own

TRRRRRrT

special Germblock
routine. He was
very creative.

Melanie was confused; she had no
idea why she'd been Germblocked.
But she knew the rules. She sighed,
put her slice of birthday cake back in
her lunch box, closed the lid, stood up,
and shuffled across the playground to
sit by herself on the steps outside the
Junior School Learning Center.

This was the Germblock
Punishment. And the Junior School
Learning Center was Germblock Jail.
A Germblock is what happens when
someone sees someone else doing
something disgusting.

 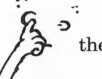 Like picking
their nose.

Or scratching
their bottom.

Or
spitting
on the
ground.

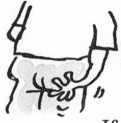

If you saw
someone do
that, you yelled,
"Germblock!"
and crossed your
arms in an X to
protect yourself from their germs.

Nobody was too sure how it worked, but it was very scientific.

And now, sitting alone in Germblock Jail, Melanie was too upset to eat her birthday cake.

What had she done to make Tamara Germblock her?

She was a clean person who would never pick her nose or scratch her bottom or spit on the ground. She didn't even understand how crossing your arms **actually** blocked germs. If that really worked, then you'd see a lot more doctors and nurses doing it in hospitals.

WHAT COULD SHE DO?

She'd just have to be patient and wait for Tamara to un-Germblock her. It might take two or three minutes, so she counted the seconds in her own special Melanie way. Using "Mister Snookies."

"One Mister Snooky, two Mister Snooky, three Mister Snooky . . ."

one Mister
SNOOKY
Two mister
snooky...

While she counted, the rest of the kids gathered around Tamara on the other side of the playground. Atticus asked the question everyone was thinking: "So, Tamara, why did we Germblock Melanie?"

Tamara gave him a very serious look. "Because she went to the bathroom and—and—she did **NOT** wash her hands!"

That didn't sound right to Debra-Jo. "Are you *sure* she didn't wash her hands? That doesn't sound like Melanie at all. She always washes her hands."

Atticus nodded. "It's true. Melanie has very clean hands."

Battie thought about the situation.

"Maybe . . . maybe it was just an accident. Maybe Melanie didn't wash her hands because she forgot. Like you know how sometimes you forget to take a shower for a few days?"

Everybody shook their heads no. Battie quickly added, "No, me neither." Then he tried to look busy, staring at the clouds in the sky.

Tamara got back to the matter at hand. "I'm telling you, Melanie absolutely did not wash her hands! When the bell rang for little lunch, we both went straight to the bathroom. Melanie finished before me and I absolutely did not hear her turn on the tap to wash her hands. So I had no choice . . . it was a definite Germblock!"

"What do you mean, you didn't *hear*?" asked Debra-Jo suspiciously.

"I mean, I was in the bathroom stall and I never heard the tap go on."

"So . . . if you were in the bathroom stall, you didn't actually *see* that she didn't wash her hands?"

"No, because there was nothing to see."

"Hmmmm," murmured Debra-Jo, strolling over to Atticus. "A very interesting story, don't you think, Atticus?"

"Hmmm," murmured Atticus right back.

"Verrry interesting."

Tamara began to fidget. Debra-Jo began to pace. Atticus began to stroke his chin. Battie began to stare at two clouds that were moving closer to each other. And Rory began to work on his Germblock routine, trying to give his monkey dance a bit more leg bounce.

While all this was going on, Melanie sat by herself in Germblock Jail, wondering when Tamara would finally come along to un-Germblock her. It was taking forever. She was already up to 312 Mister Snookies. . . .

She really wanted to eat her slice of cake, but it was too hard to eat and count at the same time.

So she just counted.

"313 Mister Snooky, 314 Mister Snooky . . ."

On the other side of the playground, Tamara was sitting on the bench, nibbling nervously on a carrot. Debra-Jo paced back and forth in front of her, her hands tucked behind her back. She'd seen lawyers walk like that on TV lawyer shows, and she figured it must be how all lawyers walk around.

"I'm confused, Tamara," she said as she paced past. "How did you know what Melanie did or didn't do if you were in the bathroom stall the whole time?"

"Yes, how *did* you know, Tamara?" Atticus began pacing with his hands behind his back because Debra-Jo was doing it, so he thought he should do it too. "It's not like you could *see* through the stall door!"

Tamara wriggled around. "Even if I could see through the stall door I wouldn't have seen Melanie washing her hands because she wasn't there and she didn't wash them!"

Debra-Jo stopped pacing and spun around to face her. "Maybe you were flushing while she was washing, *hmmmm*?"

FLUSH

"I—I—I—" Tamara tried to stand up, but Atticus gave her a look, and she sat back down on the bench.

"Yes, Tamara," he said. "Maybe your flush drowned out her handwashing and *that's* why you didn't hear."

"No! I flushed and then I opened the stall door right away! I didn't stand there and stare at the toilet flushing—I'm not a monster! I would have seen her at the sink! She wasn't there, I tell you!"

Debra-Jo strolled up to Atticus and whispered, "I think someone's starting to crack."

Atticus whispered back, "Definitely starting to crack!"

Debra-Jo nodded. Atticus
smirked. Tamara gulped. Battie
watched two clouds join up into one
bigger cloud. Rory worked on a
flappy little tongue-poke
thing that he could add to
his Germblock routine.

And far away in Germblock Jail,
Melanie continued to count . . .

"733 Mister Snooky . . .

734
Mister Snooky . . ."

She could see her friends way over
on the other side of the playground,
hanging out together, talking, having
fun. Why was she *still* Germblocked?

This wasn't fair. This wasn't right. It was boring here. Boring and lonely.

"735 Mister Snooky, 736 Mister Snooky . . ."

Back at the bench beside the redbrick wall, Atticus leaned over Tamara, casting a shadow over her face. "All right, Tamara, let's go over it one more time! You were in the stall. You heard Melanie leave. . . ."

"I've told you everything I know! I was in the stall. Melanie flushed. She left. Then there was another flush—"

Debra-Jo swiveled on her heels.

"Another flush . . .? What other flush?"

"I don't know . . ." Tamara scratched her head, trying to remember. "Someone must have been in the 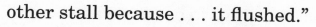 other stall because . . . it flushed."

"Who?" said Debra-Jo, getting excited. "*Who* was in the other stall?"

A long silence.

"Uhhh . . . it was me," said a voice.

Everyone turned to look at Rory.

"Well, I really had to go."

Atticus couldn't believe it. "Rory? *You* were in the girls' bathroom?

WHY WERE YOU IN THE GIRLS' BATHROOM???"

Rory had no idea what all the fuss was about. "Who wouldn't want to be in the girls' bathroom? It has that nice bubbly soap that smells like peppermint gum. The boys' bathroom just has soap that smells like floor cleaner made of horse pee. Usually I can sneak in there without anyone noticing, but this time I—"

"Wait!" Atticus interrupted. "You've been in there . . . before?"

"Yuck!" cried Debra-Jo. "That's gross and disgusting!"

"No," said Rory, "the boys' bathroom is gross and disgusting! I just wanted to use the nice girls' bathroom soap that smells like gum and then go back to class, but when I came out Melanie was still wiping her hands on her dress so I had to duck back in the stall and—"

"Melanie was **what**?" Atticus interrupted again, eyes wide open.

Debra-Jo sensed a breakthrough. "Yeah, *what*, Rory, *what*? This is super important. Tell us **exactly** what Melanie was doing."

"I told you! She was wiping her hands on her dress!"

Debra-Jo grabbed Rory's shoulders and stared into his eyes. "*Why* was she wiping her hands on her dress?"

"Because they were wet! She'd washed her hands under the tap, and she had to dry them on her dress because the hand dryer is broken!"

Debra-Jo gasped.

Atticus went "*Oooooooohhhhhh.*" Tamara looked confused. Battie watched the big cloud change back into two little clouds. Rory wondered what the problem was with him using the girls' bathroom. The girls were more than welcome to use the boys' bathroom anytime they liked.

Meanwhile, Melanie was fed up. After 975 Mister Snookies, she'd decided she'd had enough, and she stood up and walked away from Germblock Jail. She marched straight back across the playground to confront Tamara.

"Tamara!" she yelled as she got close. "I want to talk to you! I want to be un-Germblocked right now! **Germblocking is stupid and mean and totally unfair!** What kind of world are we living in if we can just exclude people because of some dumb rule? We shouldn't be excluding anybody! This should be a **Germblock-free** world!"

"OK, relax," said Tamara. She looked this way and that, avoiding Melanie's eyes.

"You're un-Germblocked."

GERMBLOCKED   UN-GERMBLOCKED

That was too easy.

"Really?" said Melanie.

"Yep, it's all over, OK?" Tamara stood up and walked away from the group, just like that.

Everyone's mouths fell open. Partly because they couldn't believe Tamara was walking away without saying sorry to Melanie. Mostly because she had a piece of toilet paper hanging out of the back of her shorts and she didn't know it was there.

GERM-
BLOCKABLE

It must have gotten stuck to her shorts when she was in the bathroom.

Toilet paper stuck to shorts deserved a full-on massive Germblock, and everyone turned to look at Melanie, waiting for her to do it.

Melanie really did want to yell

"GERMBLOCK!"

She wanted to yell it so bad.

But she remembered how horrible she felt sitting by herself in Germblock Jail, doing hundreds of Mister Snookies. Also, she couldn't really Germblock someone after giving a big speech about how people shouldn't Germblock one another anymore.

"Hey Tamara!" she yelled out.

Tamara turned around.

"Uhhh . . . you . . . you've got toilet paper stuck to your shorts!"

Tamara looked behind her and yanked off the toilet paper. Her face went bright red. She knew what was coming: Melanie was going to give her a full-on massive GERMBLOCK.

BUT IT NEVER CAME!

Instead, Melanie yelled out, "It's just toilet paper, Tamara! No big deal. See you in class!"

Tamara breathed out, feeling relieved. "OK . . . uhhh . . . thanks, Melanie. See you in class."

Melanie felt quite **proud** of herself for not doing a Germblock on Tamara. As a special reward, she opened her lunch box, got out the slice of birthday cake she'd been dreaming about all morning, brought it up to her mouth, and prepared to plunge into ultra-choco-happiness, *oh boy, oh boy, oh boy, oh*—

The bell rang. BRIIING

Rats!

For a second she thought about stuffing the whole thing into her mouth, but this cake was too amazing to rush. She put it back in her lunch box again. Closed the lid. She'd just have to wait a bit longer for ultra-choco-happiness. Until big lunch.

It ended up being a pretty disappointing little lunch for Melanie. But everyone was impressed with her for proving to them how stupid Germblocking was.

Everyone except Rory. He was really hoping to try out his whole new Germblock monkey-dance routine,

with extra-bouncy monkey dance. And added flappy tongue poke.

Danny Katz is an author and a newspaper columnist for the *Sydney Morning Herald* who is famous for his larger-than-life characters. He is the author of a number of books for children, including the Little Lunch series. Danny Katz lives in Melbourne, Australia.

Mitch Vane is the illustrator of many children's books and has also worked on storyboards, posters, package design, coloring books, cartoons, editorial illustrations, and paintings. Mitch Vane lives in Melbourne, Australia.

Don't miss the first book
in the Little Lunch series!

Rory, who forgot his lunch (again), does
something that is Really Not Allowed. Melanie
has a bake sale to help homeless puppies
(but no puppies are helped). Battie is certain
that he has ruined Grandparents Day
(but gets a surprise instead).

A lot can happen in fifteen minutes!

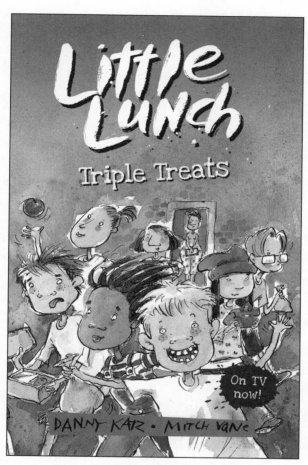

Available in hardcover